This
PJ BOOK
belongs to

_____

_____

PJ Library®

JEWISH BEDTIME STORIES and SONGS

How Dalia Put a Big Yellow Comforter Inside a Tiny Blue Box

And Other Wonders of Tzedakah

by LINDA HELLER

Illustrations by
STACEY DRESSEN
MCQUEEN

TRICYCLE PRESS
BERKELEY

Dalia liked to learn things and make things, and she did just that at the community center.

One Monday, her teacher, Mrs. Kahn, showed her and the other children a photograph of a little silver house that stood on four tiny feet.

She showed them a photograph of a miniature silver castle. She put a little wooden barrel and a small tin box on the table.

"These are tzedakah boxes," she said. "And if you make your own tzedakah box and fill it, you'll be amazed by what we can do."

When Dalia got home she ran to her room. She found a little box. She made a slot in its lid. She painted the box. Afterwards, and most importantly, she wrote the Hebrew letters *Tsadee Daled Kof Hay* on its front.

She took a dollar from her birthday money, dropped it through the slot, and placed the box on her shelf.

Her little brother, Yossi, saw the box. "What's in it?" he asked.

"A big yellow comforter," Dalia answered, with a look that said big sisters know so much more than their little brothers do.

"But how can a big yellow comforter fit into such a tiny box?" Yossi was just learning his Hebrew letters. "Is *Tsadee Daled Kof Hay* a magic word?"

"*Tsadee Daled Kof Hay* spells *tzedakah*. And it means I'm happy when you're happy," Dalia said. Not only was she Yossi's big sister but she was also his very smart teacher.

On Tuesday, Dalia earned fifty cents for weeding the garden. She took a quarter from her earnings and dropped it through the slot. "Now there's a big yellow comforter and a butterfly bush inside the box," she told Yossi.

"But how can a big yellow comforter and a butterfly bush fit inside a little box?" Yossi asked. He'd whispered *Tsadee Daled Kof Hay* to his own yellow blanket and the letters had not made it shrink. "Tell me the truth," he said. "What does *tzedakah* mean?"

"*Tzedakah* means I'm planting a kiss on your cheek," Dalia said.

On Wednesday, Dalia sold lemonade.
She slid five nickels through the slot
and listened to them fall.

"Now there's a big yellow comforter, a butterfly bush, and a banana cream pie inside the box," she told Yossi. "And I know just what you're going to ask. *Tzedakah* means we're all one big family. It means I want your wishes to come true. It means I care for you."

Yossi peered into the box. He shook it and heard the coins rattle. "It's just a bank," he said. He had his own bank and he knew not to make up lies about it.

"It's not a bank," Dalia said. "It's a tzedakah box. *Tzedakah* means fairness. It means doing the right thing. It means thinking of others and giving them what they need. Because of that, there are kisses and wishes and hugs in this box, along with a big yellow comforter, a butterfly bush, and a banana cream pie."

Yossi's lip quivered. He wanted to believe her. He loved his big sister.

"Actually," Dalia said, "my kisses and wishes and hugs are in the box along with part of the money for a big yellow comforter, a butterfly bush, and a banana cream pie. We're going to buy those things once our boxes are full. I want you to come with us."

On Thursday, Dalia and Yossi took turns carrying the little box to the community center. Other children had brought their tzedakah boxes too.

"This is my brother Yossi," Dalia announced. "I'm teaching him all about tzedakah."

Yossi helped the children count the money. At the linen store, he was the first to spot a soft yellow comforter.

At the nursery, he learned that butterfly bushes got their name because butterflies love to drink their nectar.

At the bakery, Mrs. Kahn allowed him, a
boy who was three years younger than the
other children, to place the order.
"One banana cream pie, please," he said.

Back at the community center, Mrs. Kahn passed out special markers and the children drew on the fabric. She found sprinkles and the children made hearts on the pie.

Yossi was having a wonderful time.

"Tomorrow will be even better," Dalia told him.

"How will it be better?" he asked.

"Wait and see," Dalia answered.

The next day, Mrs. Kahn led the parade of children to a house where the yard looked sad and the old woman who sat on the porch looked even sadder.

"Pay attention," Dalia whispered to Yossi. "This is the important part."

"Hello, Mrs. Ross," Mrs. Kahn called. "We've come to visit."

"What a nice surprise," Mrs. Ross said. "I've been sitting here wishing I had visitors."

The children tucked the big yellow comforter around Mrs. Ross's thin legs.

"At my age I'm usually cold," Mrs. Ross said. "But wrapped in this beautiful comforter, I feel the warmth of your hearts."

The children planted the butterfly bush where Mrs. Ross could see it. Within minutes, a flock of white butterflies flew to its blossoms.

"I've never seen anything as lovely," Mrs. Ross said. "Aside from your smiling faces."

"We're not done!" Dalia shouted.

She cut the banana cream pie. Yossi served Mrs. Ross a great big piece.

"When I woke up this morning I never guessed that today would be so grand," Mrs. Ross said. "People care about me and I won't forget that again. Thank you so very much."

"Tsadee Daled Kof Hay," Yossi sang. "Tsadee Daled Kof Hay. Tsadee Daled Kof Hay." He turned to his sister.

"I know just what you're going to ask," Dalia said. She was his big sister, his smart teacher, and she loved him very much. "And yes, as soon as we get home I'll show you how to make your own tzedakah box."

Tzedakah Boxes

The word *tzedakah* comes from the Hebrew word *tzedek*, meaning "justice" or "fairness." Many people need help and the Judaic tradition of tzedakah reminds us that it is right and just to help them. It is everyone's happy duty to help others no matter how little we have ourselves.

Two thousand years ago, the First Temple in Jerusalem needed to be repaired. The High Priest made a hole in a box, people put money in it, and the tradition of tzedakah boxes was born. As time passed, many synagogues carried on the tradition and had large tzedakah boxes of their own. Some of the money was used to keep the synagogue in good condition while the rest helped people in the community. In the 1700s, families began to keep little tzedakah boxes in their kitchens and put money in them before every meal. When Jews came to America they brought the tradition of tzedakah boxes with them. Those who spoke Yiddish called a tzedakah box a *pushkah* which means "box" or "can."

Today, many children make tzedakah boxes at Hanukkah and on their birthdays to share the coins and bills they've received with those in need. They give tzedakah on their bat or bar mitzvah. They raise money to help poor children and sick children throughout the year because they realize that every day becomes a special day when they give tzedakah. No child is ever too young to help others. Even a few pennies can be a wonderful sign of love.

For my grandmother Sarah Witkin,
who sold her jewelry to help the poor.
—L.H.

With lots of love, hugs, and kisses
to Rob, Finn, and Emma.
—S.D.M.

Text copyright © 2011 by Linda Heller
Illustrations copyright © 2011 by Stacey Dressen McQueen

All rights reserved. Published in the United States by Tricycle Press,
an imprint of Random House Children's Books, a division of Random House, Inc., New York.
randomhouse.com/kids

Tricycle Press and the Tricycle Press colophon are registered trademarks of Random House, Inc.

Library of Congress Cataloging-in-Publication Data

Heller, Linda.
How Dalia put a big yellow comforter inside a tiny blue box: and other wonders of tzedakah / by Linda Heller ;
illustrations by Stacey Dressen McQueen. — 1st ed.
p. cm.
Summary: After learning about the Jewish tradition of tzedakah boxes,
Dalia shares her knowledge with her younger brother, Yossi, by telling him what her savings can help
to provide for someone in need. Includes a note about the history and customs of tzedakah boxes.
[1. Charity—Fiction. 2. Judaism—Customs and practices—Fiction. 3. Brothers and sisters—Fiction.
4. Jews—Fiction.] I. Dressen-McQueen, Stacey, ill. II. Title.
PZ7.H37424Hp 2011
[E]—dc22
2010024325

ISBN 978-1-58246-378-0 (hardcover)
ISBN 978-1-58246-402-2 (Gibraltar lib. bdg.)
ISBN 978-1-58246-382-7 (PJ Library)

Printed in Malaysia

Design by Katie Jennings
Typeset in Hombre & Colwell
The illustrations in this book were rendered in acrylic and oil pastel.

2 3 4 5 6 — 16 15 14 13

101325K2

The Brave Little Tailor

The Brave Little Tailor

RETOLD BY
Peggy Thomson

ILLUSTRATED BY
James Warhola

SIMON & SCHUSTER BOOKS FOR YOUNG READERS
PUBLISHED BY SIMON & SCHUSTER
NEW YORK · LONDON · TORONTO · SYDNEY · TOKYO · SINGAPORE

One summer morning, a little tailor was working at his table by the window. It was a fine day, and he sewed busily. An old woman came down the street, calling, "Jam! Delicious jam for sale!"

The tailor had been working hard all morning without stopping for breakfast. He put his head out the window and shouted, "Up here, good woman, I'll buy some of your jam."

The old woman, who was rather stout, made her way up three flights of stairs with her heavy basketful of jars. When she reached his room, she unpacked the jams.

"Let me see," the tailor said, peering into every single pot, sniffing the jam and holding it up to the light. "This one looks good. I'll have half a jar of this raspberry jam, please."

The old woman had expected more from such a fussy customer, especially after she had climbed all those steps, so she grumbled a little as she filled a glass jar half way and put on a lid.

After she had left, the tailor took a knife and a loaf of bread from the cupboard. He cut off a thick slice of bread and generously spread the jam on it. "I'll just finish this jacket I'm working on and then take a break," he said, licking his lips.

The sweet smell of the jam was heavy in the air, and the tailor, looking forward to his snack, eagerly sewed faster and faster. Several flies were also attracted to the aroma, and a few of them flew down and settled on the bread.

"What's this? Who invited you?" said the tailor, swatting at them. But the flies were very hungry, and very stubborn, and they came now in even greater numbers, clinging to the sticky jam.

Finally, the little tailor, who was hungry and short-tempered, grabbed a piece of leftover cloth from his worktable and angrily swatted with all his might. When he looked down, there were seven flies stretched out dead in front of him.

"Seven at one blow! How do you like that?" he exclaimed, quite pleased with himself. He glanced around, sorry that there was nobody else in the room to witness his accomplishment.

Then he had an idea. He sat down at the table, cut a new piece of cloth, and stitched SEVEN AT ONE BLOW on the cloth in bright gold letters.

"I'll make this into a banner to hang out the window, so the townsfolk will know of my great deed," he said to himself. "Maybe it will even help business a little."

Again the little tailor set to work, humming a tune; and as the needle and thread moved in his nimble fingers, he thought, "Wait! Why just the town? I want the whole world to know of my bravery!" So he made the cloth into a vest, put it on, and admired himself in the mirror. SEVEN AT ONE BLOW was enblazoned across his back. The little tailor could hardly wait to stroll through the town.

On his way out the door, he pocketed a piece of leftover cheese that was on the counter. A tiny sparrow was perched on the sill watching him work. Thinking she would be good company, he pocketed her, too.

The tailor felt on top of the world as he walked along, passing shops and gardens and nodding to neighbors. After a while, he climbed a path that led up the side of a steep mountain.

When he reached the top and paused to catch his breath, the tailor found himself face-to-face with a giant, who was sitting on a rock. "Greetings, my tall friend," he said. "I'm off to seek my fortune on this fine day. Care to join me?"

"You?" snorted the giant. "Why, a small fry like you couldn't even keep pace with me."

"Small fry, indeed! Hmph!" said the proud tailor, swelling his chest and drawing himself up to his full height, which wasn't very high. "Read this if you think I'm so small."

The giant bent down and read, "Seven at one blow." "Hmm," he thought, "Seven what? Seven men? *Seven men!*" His eyes widened with fear, as he wondered if he had met his match. But giants have their pride, too, so he decided to test the strength of the boastful little tailor.

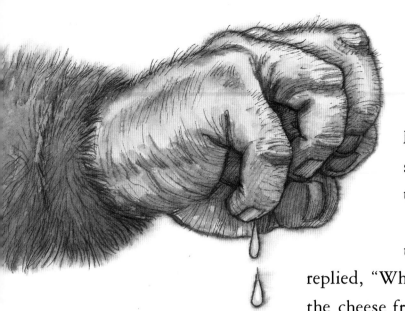

"If you can kill seven at one blow, let's see you do this." He picked up a stone and gave it such a mighty squeeze that water actually dripped out of it.

The tailor was impressed, and more than a little nervous, but quickly he replied, "Why, that's just a lark for me." He took the cheese from his pocket and pressed it until the liquid ran out.

The giant could hardly believe his eyes. He picked up another stone and threw it so far that they lost sight of it until, finally, they heard it splash into a nearby pond. "Top that, little fellow," he said, smiling.

"Not bad, not bad at all," replied the tailor. "But your stone came down again and landed in the water. What if I hurled one with such force that it never came back?"

"Ho, ho," rumbled the giant. "Don't make me laugh. A midget like you could not accomplish a feat like that."

But no sooner had he spoken than the little tailor took the bird from his pocket and threw her up in the air. Delighted to be out of the tailor's pocket and free again, the bird stretched her wings and soared into the sky.

The giant scratched his head. He was surprised at the tailor's strength, but he wasn't ready to give in. He gestured to a huge, gnarled old oak tree that was lying on the ground. "Help me carry that tree out of the forest—if you can, that is."

"Child's play!" exclaimed the tailor. "Why don't you take the trunk on your shoulders, and I'll carry the end with the branches. That's the heaviest part, after all."

With a grunt of effort, the giant hoisted up the tree and settled the huge trunk on his shoulders. Instead of carrying the other end, however, the little tailor hopped up and perched on the branches. The giant, who could not see behind him, was carrying the whole tree, and the tailor to boot. The tailor whistled a tune as the giant stumbled along under the weight. At last, the giant could go no farther and cried, "Look out, I have to let it fall!"

The tailor hopped off quickly, and before the giant could catch his breath and turn around, he grabbed hold of some branches as if he had been carrying them all along. "What a shame," he said. A hefty fellow like you and too weak to carry a tree, even with all my help!"

The giant did not say anything, but he vowed to himself that he would best the little tailor yet.

As they continued along the path together, they came upon a cherry tree. The giant took hold of the upper branches where the ripest, juiciest fruit hung, pulled down one branch, and invited the tailor to eat. But the little tailor was too weak to hold the branch; and when the giant released it, it sprang back and the tailor shot into the air as if he were shot from a cannon.

When the tailor landed with a thump on the ground several yards off, the giant boomed, "Ho, ho, what's this? Not even strong enough to hold on to a twig?"

"Silly giant," said the tailor, brushing himself off. "I leaped over those branches because I saw hunters down in the bushes and I didn't want to be a target. I bet *you* can't jump that high."

The giant tried, but he got stuck in between the branches and was left hanging there, feeling foolish. Once again, the tailor had outfoxed him.

The giant still would not give up! After he climbed down from the tree, he said, "Well now, Mr. Seven-At-One-Blow, if you're such a brave fellow, why don't you spend the night with us in the giants' cave?"

Exhausted after his day, the little tailor agreed; and soon they entered a huge cave, where several giants sat around a fire, gnawing noisily on large bones. The tailor was shown to a bed, and everyone settled down for the night.

It was a giant-size bed, however, and the tailor, accustomed to cozier lodgings, felt lost on the huge mattress. So he pulled the blanket from the bed, curled up in a nearby corner next to the fire, and quickly fell asleep.

In the middle of night, the giant, thinking the tailor was fast asleep in the huge bed, came up to it with a heavy iron poker and sliced through the mattress with one mighty blow. Finally, he thought, he had finished off the little man.

But when the giants returned from hunting for breakfast at dawn, they were surprised to see the brave little tailor calling to them from the entrance to the cave. Terrified that he would take revenge and strike them dead in one blow, they ran away as quickly as their huge bodies could go.

For the rest of the day, the little tailor continued on his way, following paths through the forests and pausing occasionally to drink from a pond. As the sun was going down, he came upon the courtyard of a royal palace. Weary from his travels, he lay down on the grass and fell asleep.

"Seeing a stranger in their midst, the townspeople began to gather around him. When they read the words "seven at one blow" on the tailor's vest, they assumed that he was a great warrior. "The king should hear of this," they said.

The king, who was always looking for brave men for his army, sent a messenger to the tailor to offer him a post. So it was that the little tailor became a soldier of high rank and was given a lovely house with servants to do his bidding. The king felt very fortunate to have found such a brave soldier to help defend his realm.

The other soldiers were not pleased, for they were afraid of the little tailor. "What if we offend him," they said, "or just *look* at him the wrong way, and he decides to fight us! Seven of us will go down in a single blow."

When the king heard of their unhappiness, he sympathized, with them, for he was a just ruler. The truth was, he felt a little sorry that he had ever set eyes on the little man. However, he was afraid of the tailor, too, and he worried that such a brave warrior would take revenge by striking him and his people dead in one blow.

That night the king thought and thought as he paced back and forth in the castle. At last he came up with a plan.

The next day the king sent for the little tailor. "My brave man, I have a request to make of you. In the forest live two fearsome giants, who cause trouble in the land with their robberies and destruction. No one who has yet attempted to battle them has survived to tell the tale. I want you to stop them. You will have one hundred of my best horsemen to assist you. If you can kill the giants, I pledge to give you my only daughter for a wife and half of the kingdom as her dowry."

"Indeed!" exclaimed the tailor. "Why, that would be a suitable match for a brave fellow like myself." And the little tailor set out, with one hundred horsemen following close behind him.

When they reached the forest of the terrible giants, he said, "Just wait here. I can take care of them alone."

The soldiers marveled at his courage.

The little tailor walked on until he spied the two giants. They lay sleeping under a tree, their great snores causing the branches to wave up and down. The clever tailor quickly gathered two pocketfuls of stones and climbed up the tree. Perching himself on a sturdy branch, he dropped one stone after another onto the chest of one of the giants.

The giant twitched and turned in his sleep. Finally he awoke, grumpily shoving his comrade and muttering, "Why are you hitting me?"

"You must be dreaming," replied the other. "I haven't touched you."

They lay down again to sleep, and the little tailor dropped some stones onto the chest of the second giant.

"What is this?" he said. "I said I wasn't hitting you!"

"I'm not doing a thing to you either," replied the first giant.

Annoyed at having their sleep disturbed, the two giants argued for some time. Finally, they became so enraged that they grabbed larger stones and pelted each other so fiercely that at last they both fell down dead.

Then the clever tailor, who had observed the battle from the safety of the branches, leaped down. Calling out to the horsemen, he said, "Fear no more. The deed is done. Even two fearsome giants were no match for the man who has killed seven at one blow."

When the little tailor returned to the palace, he asked the king for the promised reward. However, the king hesitated, for he was still thinking of ways to get rid of the little man.

"Before I give you my daughter and half of my kingdom," he said, "you must perform one more heroic deed. In the forest roams a unicorn that has done great damage. I want you to catch it."

"One unicorn is less trouble than two giants," replied the tailor. Besides, nothing is too difficult for a man who has killed seven at one blow." And he set off into the forest again, ax in hand.

Before long, the unicorn appeared, its horn gleaming in the sun. The little tailor quickly took off his vest and waved it in front of the animal. The unicorn rushed at the man, racing as fast as he could, trying to run him through with his horn.

The little tailor jumped nimbly aside, and the unicorn ran past him, ramming into a tree and driving his horn so deeply into the trunk that he could not draw it out again.

"Now I have you!" said the tailor. With his ax, he chopped off the unicorn's horn and cut the horn out of the tree. Then he triumphantly brought it to the king.

The king, however, was still hoping to rid himself of the little man, so made a third demand before giving the promised reward. Before the wedding, he said, the tailor had to catch a wild boar that was tearing up bushes in the forest.

Once again the little tailor went deep into the forest. When the boar saw him, he ran at him, gnashing his huge teeth and foaming at the mouth.

The clever tailor was standing in front of a well, however, and when the angry animal charged him, the man quickly stepped aside. The boar was running too fast to stop, and he promptly leaped over the low wall and fell into the well.

The little tailor returned to the king, who now had no choice but to take him as his son-in-law and reward him with his daughter and half of his kingdom. Had he known that this magnificent hero was really just a common tailor, he would have been even more upset. But the king was true to his word, and the wedding was held with great festivity, though little joy on the king's part.

On their wedding night, the tailor tossed and turned in his sleep, murmuring to himself. The princess pitied him, thinking that he was unaccustomed to his new surroundings. Then suddenly she heard her new husband call out, "We'll need extra fabric for these breeches, boy. Measure out another yard! Where are my scissors when I need them?" The princess was alarmed. Fearing that the poor man was ill or deranged, she shook him awake.

"Darling, you've been shouting in your sleep. What's this about scissors and fabric? Why, you were talking like a common tailor!"

The tailor was terrified. "My secret is out," he thought. "Once she finds out who I really am, she will no longer love me. I'll be ridiculed throughout the kingdom, and I'll lose everything. I'll be lucky if they don't throw me in prison!" However, he loved the princess dearly, and so told her the truth about himself.

The princess surprised him. She was not angry. She was moved that a common tailor would attempt such feats to prove himself and win her love. "Not only are you brave," she said, "but clever, as well!"

They embraced and settled down again to sleep, thinking how fortunate they were to have found each other.

Little did they know that someone else had overheard the tailor's confession. The king had been pacing the hallway and had heard the shouting. Thinking that his daughter was in danger, he ran to the bedroom door. What a shock! A common tailor marry his daughter and rule half of his kingdom?

Once again the king paced and paced until he thought of a plan to get rid of the tailor.

The next day, in the scullery, the king told the chambermaid, "Tonight when you are finished turning down the bed, leave the door slightly ajar. My guards will stand watch outside, and when he is fast asleep, they will tie him up and carry him off to a ship that will transport him to the other side of the world. That will take care of this annoying little man once and for all."

Little did the king know, however, that the chambermaid was a friend of the tailor's. (She was rather stout, and he had once made her the only uniform that fit her properly.) When the king left for his afternoon ride, she took the tailor aside and told him of the plan.

"We'll see about that!" said the tailor.

That night, he and the princess went to bed at the usual time. When the princess heard him snoring, she quietly opened the door wide so that the guards could hear clearly. The little tailor had only pretended to be asleep and now called out, "Boy, get me that extra fabric immediately, or I'll beat you with my yardstick! I killed seven at one blow, finished off two giants, chopped off the unicorn's horn, and captured a wild boar. Why should I be afraid of those who are standing outside my room now?"

When they heard this, the guards fled in fear. None of them dared attack a man who was so brave and clever.

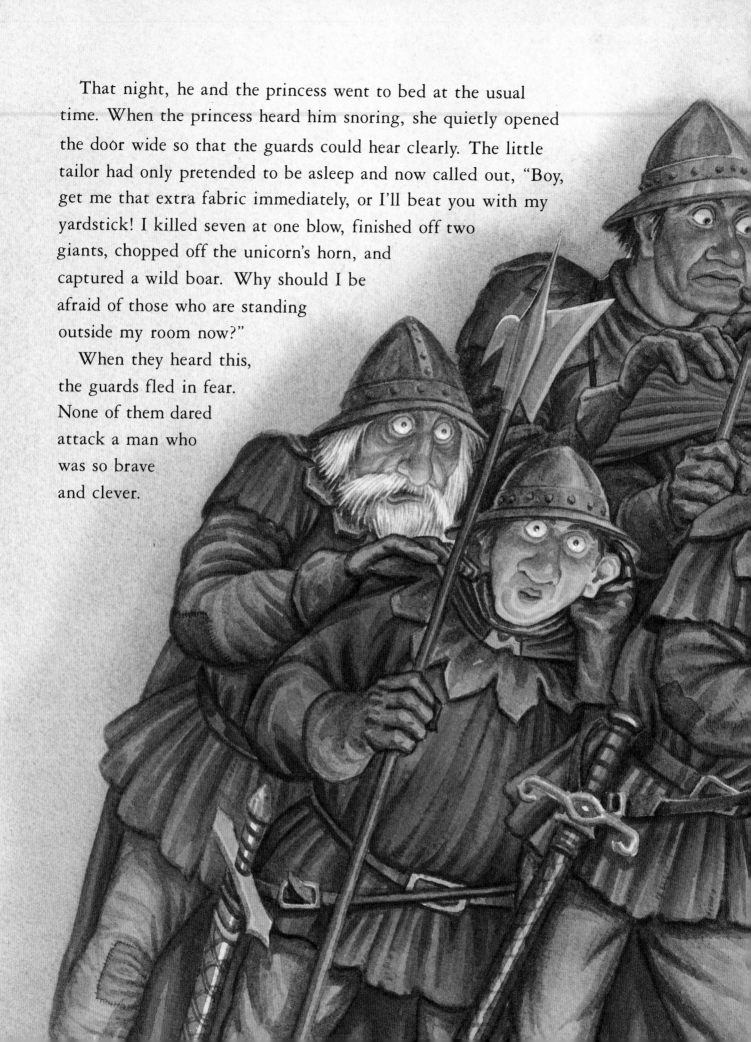

And from that time on the little tailor lived
happily with the princess.

SIMON & SCHUSTER BOOKS FOR YOUNG READERS
Simon & Schuster Building, Rockefeller Center
1230 Avenue of the Americas, New York, New York 10020.
Text copyright © 1992 by Peggy Thomson. Illustrations copyright © 1992 by James Warhola.
SIMON & SCHUSTER BOOKS FOR YOUNG READERS is a trademark of Simon & Schuster.
Designed by Lucille Chomowicz.
The text of this book is set in Garamond #3.
The illustrations were done in watercolor.
The display type was hand-lettered by John Stevens.
Manufactured in Hong Kong 10 9 8 7 6 5 4 3 2 1

Library of Congress Cataloging-in-Publication Data
Thomson, Peggy.   The brave little tailor / retold by Peggy Thomson; illustrated by James Warhola.
Summary: A tailor who kills seven flies with one blow outwits the king and earns half his kingdom
and his daughter's hand in marriage.   [1. Fairy tales.   2. Folklore—Germany.]   I. Warhola, James, ill.
II. Title.   PZ8.T377Mr   1992   398.2—dc20   [E]   CIP 91-20982
ISBN 0-671-73736-8